For Jan Mark, and James and Joe—with love
—S.P.

For Maggie Mundy
—P.H.

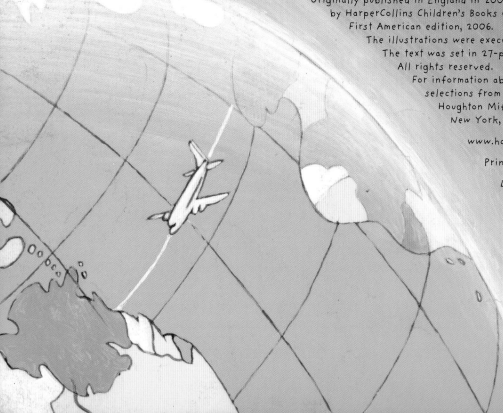

Clarion Books
a Houghton Mifflin Company imprint
215 Park Avenue South, New York, NY 10003
Text copyright © 2005 by Simon Puttock
Illustrations copyright © 2005 by Philip Hopman
Originally published in England in 2005
by HarperCollins Children's Books under the title *Stella to Earth!*
First American edition, 2006.
The illustrations were executed in pastels, crayons, and paint.
The text was set in 27-point ProvidenceAlt-Medium.

www.houghtonmifflinbooks.com

Printed in Singapore

Library of Congress Cataloging-in-Publication Data
Puttock, Simon.
[Stella to Earth!]
Earth to Stella! / by Simon Puttock ; illustrated by Philip Hopman.
—1st American ed.
p. cm.
Originally published: England : Collins, 2005 under the title Stella to Earth!
Summary: Before Stella's father comes in to tell her a bedtime story,
Stella takes a little trip in a spaceship.
ISBN-13: 978-0-618-58535-9   ISBN-10: 0-618-58535-4
[1. Bedtime—Fiction. 2. Space flights—Fiction.] I. Hopman, Philip,
ill. II. Title.
PZ7.P9835Ear 2006
[E]—dc22   2005021168

10 9 8 7 6 5 4 3 2 1

EARTH TO STELLA!

by Simon Puttock
Illustrated by Philip Hopman

Clarion Books
New York

"Time for bed, Stella," said Dad. "As soon as you're settled, I'll be back to tell you a story. What sort of story would you like?"

"A space story, please," said Stella.

Stella brushed her
teeth and washed
her face. Then she
climbed into her
stripy space suit.

"EARTH TO STELLA: DON'T FORGET TO SCRUB BEHIND YOUR EARS!" Dad called.

"CHECK!" said Stella, because that's what astronauts say when they mean yes.

Stella stepped into her spaceship
and twisted her helmet on tight.
Then she counted backwards,

5...

4...

3...

2...

1...

BLAST OFF!

The spaceship WHOOMPHED into the sky.

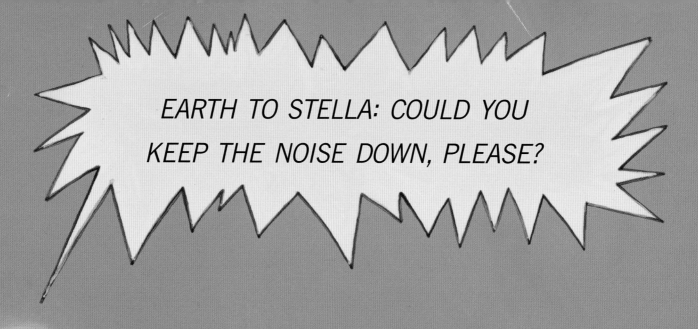

Stella zoomed toward the Moon.
She landed in a crater. The Moon was
very good for bouncing, so she bounced
up and down by the Earth's eerie light.

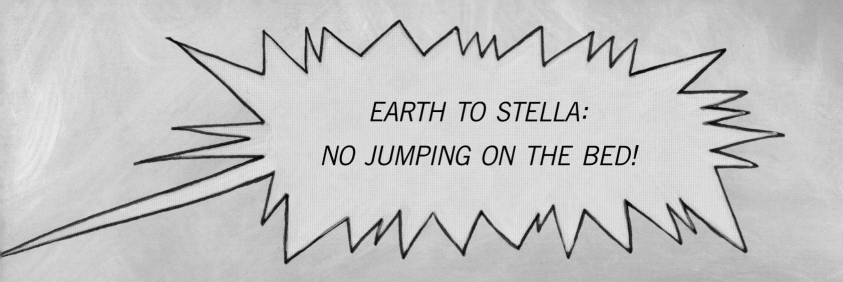

Back in her spaceship, Stella revved
the engine and headed out through the solar
system, toward deep space and new stars.

EARTH TO STELLA: ARE YOU TUCKED IN TIGHT?

Up close, each star was like
the Sun, huge and round and hot.

14

Some stars burned bluish white, others flamed yellow, and some bloomed rose red. Stella liked the red stars best.

15

A comet whizzed by, trailing a
long, fiery tail. It was wonderful
to watch, but a bit scary, too.
"Zikes!" said Stella,
and she zoomed away.

17

Stella found a beautiful
planet spinning like
a jewel around a little
yellow sun. She decided
to land on it. WHOOOSH.

The spaceship touched down . . .

. . . and Stella stepped outside.

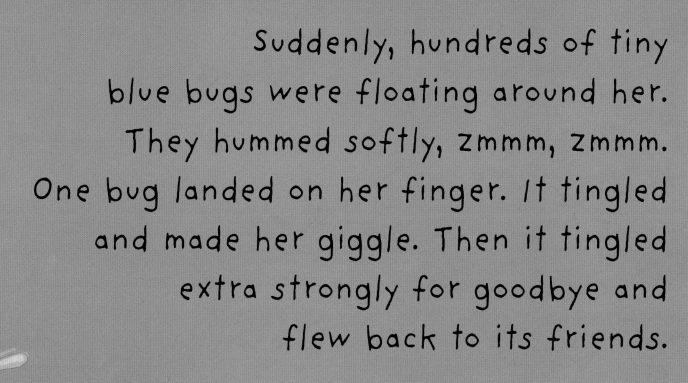

Suddenly, hundreds of tiny
blue bugs were floating around her.
They hummed softly, zmmm, zmmm.
One bug landed on her finger. It tingled
and made her giggle. Then it tingled
extra strongly for goodbye and
flew back to its friends.

But Earth did not answer.

No reply.
Suddenly, Stella DID feel alone.

"I have to go now," Stella said.
"But I'll be back soon. Goodbye, blue bugs!"

Stella zoomed back
through the galaxy . . .

28

. . . and landed safely in her bedroom.
STELLA TO EARTH: I'M BACK!

But there was still no reply.
Worried, Stella set off to explore
her home planet.

Dad was in the living room.
He was snoring gently.
"Wake up, earthling!" said Stella. "It's me."
"So I see," said Dad. "And it's past your—"

"Bedtime?" said Stella. "I know, but could we go and visit my new friends first?"
"What new friends are those?" asked Dad.
"Space friends!" said Stella. "In outer space."
"Zikes!" said Dad. "I'll get my space helmet."